THE
SECRET ROOM

BY CYNTHIA MERCATI

Cover Illustration: Paul Micich
Inside Illustration: Deb Bovy

CONTENTS

1

A Minister's Daughter

Sometimes it's hard to be the daughter of a minister. (We call a minister a *dominee* in Holland.) People expect you to be quiet in church and extra-smart in school. They also think you should be good and polite all the time. I'm just not made that way!

First of all, I have a terrible time keeping quiet—anywhere! I just have to say what I'm thinking, even if it gets me in trouble. Which it usually does.

Secondly, I'm not very good at my studies. I'm okay at history. But as for math and science, I'm hopeless. I only get through them because my best friend, Leah, helps me with my homework.

And lastly, I'm not very well-behaved. Just ask my mother! She says that sometimes I shout so much, I give her a headache.

She also says that I never walk when I can run. That my room is always messy. And that my hair is never brushed.

And Mama's right! The world is such an exciting place. There's so much I want to see and do that it seems silly to waste all that time on being neat.

Mama often says, "If only you could be more like Siri!"

Siri is my older sister. She has blond hair as smooth and shiny as silk. And her eyes are as blue as our Dutch sky on a cloudless day.

My hair, on the other hand, is dishwater blond. And my eyes are much more gray than blue.

Siri's blouses are always tucked neatly into her pleated skirts. And her collars and cuffs are always white and shining.

My shirttails are always hanging out. The hems on

my skirts are always unraveling. And my shoes are usually scuffed.

Siri has a gentle smile and a very ladylike way of walking and talking. She sings in the church choir and makes the best grades in her high school. And when people in Papa's church are sick, Siri's the first one to visit them.

When she isn't helping Mama in the kitchen or out doing good deeds, Siri's doing needlework. People are forever saying, "Siri's handiwork is prettier than anything you can buy in the shops!"

Mama tried to teach me the delicate sewing that Siri's so good at—once. My hands just don't work that way. And besides, I can't sit still that long. I always seem to have a case of the fidgets. At church, school, or home, I always have to be on the move.

"A young lady should learn to sit quietly," Mama is forever telling me.

But Papa sticks up for me. "Leave Annie be," he'll say. "She has energy to burn, and that's a good thing!"

He always smiles at me then. He takes the pipe from his mouth. And he uses it to make a little swooshing gesture toward the door, saying, "Run outside, Annie, and see the world!"

I always laugh when Papa says that. But Mama just shakes her head and makes a clucking sound. And as I run out the door, she usually makes a remark about my manners too. Or lack of them!

One time I heard her say, "Whatever will become of that child? The teachers say she rushes around all the time in school too. That's why she doesn't do as well as Siri."

"She's not Siri," Papa answered patiently. And I could have kissed him for his answer. Except I was supposed to be off playing and not eavesdropping.

Unfortunately, I eavesdrop a lot. Snooping, Mama calls it. That's how I happened to hear her say, "Annie's never going to find a husband. What with the way that she behaves and looks so untidy! And then what will she do?!"

My cheeks burned scarlet at Mama's words. Is that what it took to find a husband? I thought. Being neat and walking with prim little steps? If it did, then I definitely didn't want one!

"Maybe Annie will do something besides get married," Papa said.

"Like what?" Mama demanded.

I'd been crouched on the landing, listening. And now I ran into the living room. The words burst out of me. "There're all kinds of things I could do!" I exclaimed. "Maybe I'll own a boat—and be an explorer!"

"Don't be ridiculous," Mama said. She didn't even look up from her darning. "Girls don't do things like that."

"Then I'll be the first," I insisted. "Remember at summer camp last year? I won three medals for sailing!"

"I wasn't very happy with that camp," Mama said. "They should have been teaching you useful things. Like cooking and sewing."

"I think Annie should become a spy," Papa said with a sly smile. "She seems to be very good at overhearing things she shouldn't."

Mama only clucked her tongue at Papa's obvious joke. But her unspoken words hung heavily in the room. Like they seemed to hang over everything I did. *"If only you could be more like your sister!"*

Yes, it's hard enough being a minister's daughter—without having to be the sister of an angel too.

Our family lives in a little town very close to Amsterdam, the biggest city in Holland. But then, Holland is so small, no place is very far away from any other place. I sometimes think that in the whole universe, our little Holland must be no more than a dot.

Three rivers run right through all of Holland. They're all on their way to the North Sea. The Rhine, the Wall, and the Maas. Those rivers connect with other smaller rivers. And they all connect up with the canals that crisscross our country as straight and narrow as rulers. A canal runs right through the center of our little town.

I love to watch the boats pass by. And I love the water! I love its changing colors and its fresh, crisp scent. I love how you can swim in it and fish during the summer. And how in the winter you can skate on its frozen silver surface.

After camp I tried to tell my family how wonderful it had been to be on the water every day. And to think that by following the canals and the rivers, you could find your way to the sea. From there, you could go anywhere! Even as far as America!

"Now it's time to find your way to the sink and the dishes," Mama had replied, cutting off my words in middream. Just as she always did.

I stood up, scraping my chair against the floor with more energy than was needed. I marched over to the sink.

My mind was in a blaze of rebellion. How could Mama be like that? Maybe she was happy going no farther than the end of her nose. But I wanted adventure! Someday I was going to see the whole world!

But right now I have to be happy just exploring our little town. I usually do that with Leah.

Leah and I are in seventh grade. We've been best friends since—well, since we can remember!

Sometimes the two of us walk far into the country. And when we do, I like to lie back in the long grass and just stare up at the sky.

10

At times I feel like the very blue of the sky, the very gold of the sun, and the very scent of the wind are all inside me. And I'm a part of everything—earth, wind, and water.

Once I told Leah I wished I could just bottle up the moment and my feelings. That way I could carry them with me always.

"You can," Leah had said. "Your memories are always with you!"

That's why Leah's my best friend. She always understands!

There really aren't any unknown places in our little town to search out. No caves or woods. Like the rest of Holland, we're a flat, marshy kind of place. Nothing but land and canals stretching out in all directions.

So Leah and I just pretend we're somewhere else. Running down the banks of the Amazon. Or climbing Mount Everest. Or scaling the Pyramids.

There are good things about Holland too. Like the water and the trees! Our trees are all up and down the canals. Lindens and elms, chestnut and cherry trees.

We have plenty of birds too. Swans on the canal, ducks in the river, sparrows on the roof. And the seagulls are everywhere! They swoop down and hover over the water. Then they take off again.

I told Siri once that I thought it would be wonderful to fly. Like a seagull.

"I think it would be frightening," she said.

"But wouldn't you like to go places you've never been?" I asked. Then I whirled around the room. "Someday Leah and I are going to go to every exciting place in the world!" Names I knew only from maps rolled off my tongue. "To Zanzibar and Morocco! And Timbuktu!"

"I like it here," Siri had said quietly. "I guess I'm just a homebody, Annie."

Our village rises up on both sides of the canal. All of the houses are very much alike. Tall and narrow and made of good Dutch brick.

Our houses are always clean—and I mean always! Dutch housewives pride themselves on their cleanliness. But Mama goes a step past that, I think. She and Siri are always cleaning or polishing something.

We have a busy house too. It's right next door to Papa's church. And people are always stopping in. Happy people who want to talk about weddings or baptisms. Sad people who want to talk about funerals. People with big problems and small ones. They all want a kind listener and a bit of advice.

Papa's often late for dinner because he's been visiting people that are too old or ill to come to church. Sometimes people who don't even know us come calling at our house. But they've been told how kind Papa is and that he never turns anyone away. And he doesn't!

If people need food, that's what they get. If they need money, Papa arranges for them to talk to someone about getting jobs. He insists that the soup kettle and the coffeepot always be on. That way, the people who drop in will feel like they're welcome.

I'm glad I have Papa. And I'm glad, too, that he loves me. Because I seem to spend a lot of time feeling like I should be more like Siri and less like me.

It bothers me sometimes at night when I lie in bed. I wish that people would make comments about me like they do about my sister.

"Her hair is like spun gold!" That's what people are always saying about Siri. Or, "Look, her eyes are the color of blue china!"

All people ever say to me is, "Comb your hair! Don't talk so much! Don't run so fast! Careful—you're going to knock that over!"

Sometimes I complain to Papa. "I seem to get into an awful lot of trouble," I tell him.

He always answers the same way. "You're just as you should be, Annie," he says. "You were made the way you are for a reason."

I can't imagine what that reason might be. But maybe someday I'll find out.

In the meantime I ride my bike. I have small adventures with Leah and pretend they're big ones! And, like everyone else in Holland, I try not to worry about what Germany might be up to.

It all started when Hitler was elected chancellor of Germany. He took what used to be a perfectly nice country and turned it into a bad one. Then he ordered his soldiers to march into Poland, Czechoslovakia, and Austria and take them over too!

England and France have declared war on Germany. Maybe they'll be able to keep Hitler in his place. But it doesn't look good. In fact, Papa has told us Germany is winning the war.

When I think of Hitler and his German Reich, I get angry—and scared. So I try not to think about him. But he's getting harder and harder to ignore. He's gobbling up more and more countries. And Germany is Holland's next-door neighbor . . .

2

THE INVASION

I sat bolt upright in bed. A brilliant flash lit up the night. Then another. The sky outside my window was glowing red!

An explosion shook the bed. I could feel the house swaying around me. Plaster dust fell from the ceiling. There was another explosion. This one sounded louder and closer than the first.

The door burst open, and Mama and Siri rushed into the room. Mama's hair was sticking out wildly in all directions. Her robe was half on and half off. Never before had I seen my mother when she wasn't perfectly tidy.

Siri's silken hair was swinging loose. And her nightgown was swirling around her slender frame. We huddled together on my bed.

"What's going to happen to us?" Mama cried. She grabbed Siri's hand and mine. "What will become of us?"

There was another explosion. So loud it seemed as if the house would shake right off its foundation.

Mama buried her head in her hands. Siri and I tried to comfort her. She started sobbing, "Why don't they stop? I can't stand it!"

Papa appeared at the door. He wore a robe over his pajamas and still held his pipe in his hand.

Mama threw herself against him. "Peter, I'm so scared! Make it stop!" she screamed.

Papa patted Mama's back, making little hushing noises. "It's the Germans," he said. "It just came over the radio. They've invaded Holland. They're bombing Amsterdam."

Siri and I ran to Papa. And all three of us clung to him. We were like drowning people. And he was our life preserver.

"We have to get downstairs," he commanded as the

explosions became even louder. "It's safer there!"

As if to prove the truth of his words, the force of the next explosion broke the window. Glass flew everywhere. I screamed and fell to my knees as glass and wood hurtled through the air. Papa pushed Siri and Mama to the floor.

"What will become of us?" Mama moaned again and again.

"Downstairs!" Papa yelled. I crawled into the hallway, and Siri followed me. But Mama was rocking back and forth on her knees, her arms folded around her middle.

It made me feel a little strange to see my strong, sure mother like a helpless child. But Papa put one arm around her waist, one hand under her arm, and pulled her to her feet. As he urged her down the stairs, I could still hear her wounded words. "What will become of us?"

When we reached the first floor, Papa gathered us in the center of the living room. He made sure we were as far away from the windows as possible.

Papa turned on the radio. The announcer's voice cut in and out. "Holland is at war," the voice crackled. "Germany is trying to conquer our country. But the Dutch army is fighting back bravely!"

Our soldiers were brave. But, still, our army was small. And they were going up against the greatest war machine in the world!

All of us had watched the newsreels that showed thousands and thousands of Nazi soldiers parading in front of Hitler. And he stood on the reviewing stand, his arm raised in a salute. Behind the soldiers had come the tanks and trucks, while the fighter planes flew overhead. The Nazis had so many weapons. So much power.

The static got so bad we couldn't hear a word the announcer was saying. Then Papa turned the radio off.

Outside, the world was an eerie color filled with fire and smoke. The explosions mixed with the rapid rhythm of machine guns. Surely there could be nothing left standing in Amsterdam by now!

Siri's face was dead white, lit by the explosions. Mama looked frozen. Her eyes were wide and staring—at nothing. Or maybe she was seeing the end of her world.

I clutched at Papa's arm. "There must be something we can do," I said. "Instead of just huddling here like frightened sheep!"

In spite of his own worry and fear, Papa gave me a smile. "You're very practical, Annie. And you are right. There is always something to be done. And what we must do now is pray," he said.

He got on his knees. Siri and I did the same. Gently, Papa helped Mama onto her knees. We all folded our hands and bowed our heads. "We must pray for our country," he said, "and her people. And our soldiers."

Brave little Holland held out against Germany for five days. During those days our home was crowded with people. They were crying, praying, and asking Papa what he thought would happen. What they wanted to hear, of course, was that we had defeated the Germans and the war was over. But not even Papa could give them that miracle.

No one went to school or work. And Mama kept Siri and me busy feeding our visitors. Mama said my fingers were just too clumsy to do any of the cooking or baking. But maybe I couldn't do much damage as a server. And I didn't. Well, not much damage. After I dropped the second tray, Mama gave me another job.

One morning a heavy roaring in the sky woke us all up. I was sleeping with Siri now. And quickly, I jumped out of bed and looked out the window.

Row after row of airplanes were flying so low, it seemed as if they'd crash into the rooftops. Siri came to stand behind me. Suddenly, the blue of the sky was dotted with what looked like giant snowflakes.

"Siri," I whispered, "those are parachutes! Thousands of German soldiers are parachuting into Holland!"

It really was hopeless. The next thing we heard on the radio was that the queen and the rest of the Dutch royal family had escaped to England. And then . . . we heard the news of the surrender.

The German Occupation Forces entered our town. Our first order came from a Nazi shouting through a big bullhorn. We were to gather in the town square to watch them.

There we all stood, no one smiling, as the soldiers marched by. As they marched, they sang a German song of triumph. "*Lift the banners high!*"

Right through our town square they came. Right where we bought our vegetables and our tulips and roses. Down our main street they came, their guns over their shoulders. Swinging their outstretched legs high in the air. Goose stepping. That's what we called the way the Nazis marched.

I felt as if I couldn't stand one more minute of their singing. Or the mocking sound of their boots striking the pavement. My eyes stung with tears of fury.

And then I did it. I deliberately turned my back on the square.

"Annie!" Mama gasped in alarm. "What are you doing? Do you want to get us all in trouble?" She put her hand on my shoulder, trying to turn me. But I dug in my heels. "Turn around right now," Mama hissed. But I shook my head.

They can make me stand here, I thought. But they can't make me watch. No one can. Not even Mr. Hitler himself!

When we returned to the house, I stood rebelliously in the front yard. I was thinking about the Germans and the world. And how wrong everything was.

Mama and Siri had already gone into the house. Not even Hitler could keep Mama from her housework!

I stared up at the wild cherry tree. There were only a few flowers left. Its fallen petals formed a carpet of white under my feet.

Beside me, Papa picked off one of the few blossoms that still clung to the tree. He held it in the palm of his hand and looked at it.

"It's amazing, isn't it, how this little flower has hung on through wind and rain—and bombs. Nothing could shake it loose," he said and looked at me. "That's how we must be now. No matter what happens, we can't give up."

Papa placed the flower in my hand. "Keep it, Annie, to remember this day," he said.

I looked at him, puzzled. "To remember the day the Nazis marched into our town?" I asked.

Papa shook his head. "No, of course not," he said. He gently closed my fingers around the petals. "Ever since Hitler came to power in Germany, we've lived in fear of him. But now—now a new day has started. Now we can start to hope. And begin to fight against him! That's what I want you to remember."

Papa turned and walked up the steps into the house. Just then a bird landed in the cherry tree and began singing at the top of its lungs. The Germans can't silence our birds, I thought. And maybe . . . they won't be able to silence us either.

I started into the house, my hand clenched carefully around the white flower of hope.

3

The Yellow Star

"THIS IS WHAT I WANT TO SAY
NAZIS, NAZIS GO AWAY!
HERR HITLER'S A BIG, FAT SWINE
YOU CAN HAVE THE ROPE NEXT TIME!"

"Annie Van Vries!" The teacher grabbed the jump rope out of my hands. "Have you gone crazy, singing that song?"

"It's just to keep time when we jump rope," I answered.

Mrs. Van Kooten lifted her head. She squared her shoulders as if coming to attention. "The Nazis are our conquerers. We must respect them!" she scolded. "We must not sing or say bad things about them—ever!" She raised one eyebrow and glared at me. "Do you understand?"

I could barely make myself say the words, "Yes, Mrs. Van Kooten."

"Very good then," Mrs. Van Kooten said. Her voice was crisp. "I will keep your jump rope until tomorrow so I'm sure you've learned your lesson." She darted a quick look at Leah. "And one more thing. You and Leah will no longer be desk partners," she said.

Quickly, I opened my mouth to protest. But Mrs. Van Kooten cut me off. "The Nazis have ordered us to separate the Jewish children from the Christian children," she said. Then she paused and bit her lip.

For a moment it looked like she was sorry. As if maybe her manner and her words were all an act. Just in case she was being watched by one of the Nazi soldiers who patrolled our streets.

But then Mrs. Van Kooten snapped back to attention. "After recess, Leah, take your books and papers to the back of the room. That is where the Jewish students will sit from now on," she instructed.

Mrs. Van Kooten marched back into the school. She slapped my jump rope sharply against her palm as she went.

I looked at Leah. Her head was down, and her lips trembled.

How dare the Nazis treat her like this! "It's not fair," I said. My voice was low and thick with anger. "It's not right! But it doesn't mean anything—we can still be best friends!" I said.

Leah looked up. Her brown eyes were brimming with tears. "It's just going to get worse and worse for the Jews," she said. "Just like in Germany! The Nazis made all these rules and laws about Jews. They made their lives horrible. And that's what's going to happen here!"

Leah dashed away the tears that spilled down her cheeks with the back of one hand. "You don't understand how it feels to be Jewish, Annie. You can't!" she cried. "There's no safe place in the world for us!"

And with that, Leah started running. Across the playground and down the street. Farther and farther until she'd disappeared from sight. Running like a wild thing. As if trying to escape from the future that waited for her.

I didn't know if she was right. That in the whole world, no place was safe for her. But I knew she was right about Holland. The Nazis were making it very clear just what they had in mind for the Jews. The first thing I started noticing were the signs.

"JODEN VERBODEN!" That's what they said. "JEWS FORBIDDEN!"

And they were posted all over. In restaurants, stores, the ice cream parlor, and the one movie theater in our village. Jews, it seemed, were no longer allowed to go anywhere.

I was with Papa when we saw the big banner the Nazis had put up in the village square. It proclaimed all kinds of new rules.

Before the war Papa and I had taken lots of walks together. We always stopped for an ice cream cone or a soda when the weather was warm. Or a steaming mug of hot chocolate when it was cold.

But now Papa was busier than ever. And when he was home, he was often shut away in his study. Talking with people I didn't know.

Once when I walked by his closed study door—I wasn't *exactly* snooping—I could hear Papa and his friends talking in hushed voices. And I wondered, what was so secret that they had to speak in whispers even behind a closed door?

On this day Papa and I were walking and talking. Not about anything big or important. Just about the little things I loved to share with him.

Then, on a lamppost in the middle of the square, we saw a huge sign. It was covered with lots of writing in big, bold black letters. Frightening letters. And horrible words.

JEWS ARE FORBIDDEN:

To go swimming!

To enter public parks!

To sit on public benches!

To own automobiles!

To own bicycles!

To own radios!

To ride on buses!

To ride on trains!

To leave their homes before 6:00 in the morning and after 6:00 at night!

Jews will no longer be issued ration cards!

As I read the sign, a sick feeling crept into my stomach.

"I don't understand, Papa," I said. "If the Jews aren't given ration cards anymore, how will they get food? We need our cards to buy groceries."

"They won't get food," Papa answered in a short, hard voice I didn't recognize as his.

I couldn't make any sense of this. "But then—then they'll starve!" I cried.

"Exactly," Papa said in that voice that was like a slap. "If the Nazis don't think of another way to kill them first!"

I had only seen Papa angry a few times in my life. And then it had been only a mild kind of anger. Like when I accidentally broke the milk pitcher that had belonged to his mother. Or when I refused to go bed when I should.

But now he was standing stock-still in front of the sign. Two red spots appeared on either side of his face. His hands had tightened into fists. And his jaw was clenched so hard, it was quivering.

He tore the sign off the post and threw it to the ground. Then he stamped on it, his footsteps as hard and angry as his voice had been. I hoped a soldier wasn't watching.

Without a word, Papa turned and walked out of the square. He walked with fast, furious strides. I hurried after him.

"You know why I did that, don't you, Annie?" Papa asked.

"Of course!" I said. "Because the Nazis have no right to march in here and tell people what to do!"

Papa stopped and put a hand on my shoulder. His face was very serious.

"That's part of it," he said. "And also because every person has the right to live in this world with his head held high. The Nazis are trying to take that away from the Jews. They're trying to make them feel less than human!"

I looked up at the man I admired more than anyone else in the world. And I saw that the blue eyes that were always so honest and clear were clouded now with pain. I covered his hand with mine.

"But we won't let them do that, will we, Papa?" I said quietly.

My father smiled then. A sad little smile that tugged at my heart.

"No," he said, "we won't!"

We started walking again. "You always do or say something that amazes me, Annie. Yes, it's like I've always said, you were made for a very special purpose," Papa praised.

"More special than driving my teacher crazy?" I asked. "Or tearing Mama's best lace curtains?"

Papa laughed. "Definitely more special than that!" he declared.

Papa frowned then, the crease between his eyebrows growing deeper. It was funny. I hadn't noticed that Papa even had any wrinkles before the Nazis came. Now they seemed to grow deeper every day.

"These are the kinds of times that make everyone wonder what their purpose is," Papa said. He was very serious. "And what they're made of."

The Nazis weren't through giving commands. Their next order was that all Jews had to wear a big yellow Star of David pinned to their clothes whenever they left the house. To be Jewish and caught on the street without your star meant imprisonment!

It was the first morning all the Jews were supposed to have their star on. And I appeared at breakfast with a clumsy Star of David I'd made out of yellow construction paper. I had pinned it to my sweater with a safety pin. As I slid into my chair at the kitchen table, Mama and Siri stared at me.

"And just what is that?" Mama asked, pointing at my very badly drawn star.

"If Leah has to wear a star, then I'm going to wear one too!" I declared.

Siri lowered her eyes and kept right on eating her cereal. She never got involved in the arguments Mama and I had.

Then Mama slapped my hand, hard, on the table. "Take that off immediately!" she ordered.

"But, Mama," I pleaded. "I want to make Leah feel better. I want to show all the Jewish children in our school I'm still their friend!"

"And what will you be showing the Nazis?" Mama asked. "Have you thought of that?"

"I don't care what the Nazis think!" I shouted back with more force than I meant to use. "It's a stupid order!"

Mama's lips tightened. "Take off that star," she ordered.

"I won't," I said flatly, glaring at Mama. I felt like a two-year-old. Like a silly infant having a temper tantrum! But I couldn't give in. This was important. Somehow, someway, I had to show the world how I felt.

"Siri, look at your sister," Mama said. But Siri didn't raise her head. "She has her mule face on!" Mama continued.

Mama folded her arms. "Well, I can be just as stubborn as you, Annie. You will go to your room and remain there until you take off the star!" she ordered.

My eyes widened in surprise. And even Siri snuck an amazed peek at Mama. "You mean you want me to miss school?" I asked.

"No, of course I don't! But do you know what could happen to you if the Nazis caught you parading around wearing that silly thing? They could arrest you! They could—" Mama broke off. And I saw that the anger in her eyes had suddenly become a fear so deep she couldn't even speak of it.

Mama turned away. "Go to your room, Annie," she said.

I stood up, so angry I accidentally knocked over Siri's juice glass. Quickly, Siri grabbed her napkin and started blotting up the juice.

"It's okay," she whispered. "I'll clean it up."

I knew it was nice of her to cover for me. But it just pointed out how perfect my sister was—and how imperfect I was!

"Of course you will," I hissed at Siri under my breath. "Anything to get in Mama's good graces."

Siri didn't answer. But I saw her flush red.

Mama whirled around. "I heard that," she snapped, "and let me tell you—"

"You don't have to tell me anything. I already know what you're going to say!" I spat out the words in a nasty, mocking voice. "Why can't you be more like your sister?!"

"Well," Mama asked, "why can't you?"

"Because I can only be what I am!" I shouted. "And I can only do what I believe in!" I clenched one hand into a fist and pounded at the clumsy yellow construction paper star. "And that means wearing this!"

Papa appeared at the door. He had his pipe in one hand and a paper sack in the other. "Apologize to your mother, Annie, for speaking to her in such a tone," Papa ordered.

I looked at the floor. I was so furious—at Mama, the Nazis, and Siri. And I was so ashamed to be scolded by Papa, I could feel my ears burning.

"I'm sorry I shouted at you, Mama," I mumbled.

"The way Annie spoke was wrong," Papa continued. "But *what* she said—about the star—was right," Papa said. He put down his pipe and pulled four bright yellow flowers from inside the sack.

"I bought these from a flower seller this morning. One for each of us to wear," Papa said. And he began fastening one of the flowers to the lapel of his jacket.

"It's my answer to the yellow Star of David the Jews have been ordered to wear," he explained. "It's like Annie said, we must show the Nazis we support our Jewish brothers and sisters. When I see a Jewish person today, I'm going to call out a greeting at the top of my lungs!"

I pulled off my star and pinned on one of the flowers. The yellow petals stood out sharply against the brown of my sweater. I felt proud. I had done something right—Papa had said so!

But Mama was pressing her hands to her face. "If the Nazis see Annie wearing that flower, they might let her off for being a silly child. But if they see you wearing one . . . you're a grown man and a leader in this town. If they hear you speaking to Jews, it could be hard for you!" she said.

"It could," Papa said without fuss. He sat down and poured himself a cup of coffee. "But it's all I know to do. We must let the Jews know we, at least, are still human beings." He paused. "And so are they."

I repeated Papa's words to myself. It was like he had said in the square. The Nazis were trying to make the Jews feel less than human. But we weren't going to let them do it!

To my surprise, I saw Siri reach across the table for a flower. She was wearing her long hair in two braids that day. And she looked like a picture in a fairy tale book. Like Snow White or Sleeping Beauty. Expertly, she twisted the flower through her hair. Papa smiled at her and nodded. And I smiled too.

For once, Siri and I were standing together. As if that was the last straw, Mama picked up the remaining yellow flower. And with quick, jerky movements, she tore it up. Then she opened her hands and let the shredded petals fall to the floor.

4

The Good-Bye

"JEW, JEW, UGLY MOLE!
STICK YOUR FACE IN A BOILING HOLE!"

"Stop singing that song! Stop it!" I flew at the two Nazi soldiers like a small tornado. And I began beating at them with my fists. But the blows landed harmlessly against their heavy coats.

"She's a fierce one all right," one of the soldiers said, chuckling. He grabbed my arm and held me in a hard grip.

No matter how I twisted and struggled, it was no use. The other soldier began singing at Leah again. He was backing her up against the brick wall of the school.

"JEW, JEW, UGLY MOLE!
STICK YOUR FACE IN A BOILING HOLE
STICK YOUR FACE IN A BOILING POT
BY TOMORROW JEW WILL ROT!"

The soldier ended the song with his face right in Leah's. And then he spit at her. He spit at my best friend!

I turned beet red, yelling out, "You have no right to insult my friend like that!"

The soldier that was holding me yanked me toward him. "Jews are unclean. Don't you know that? And greedy and mean!" he said.

"That's not true!" I shouted. The soldier gave my arm a twist. It hurt so much that my eyes watered.

"I'm warning you, little girl," the soldier growled at me. "If you want to stay out of trouble, stop hanging around with these dirty Jews!"

I looked down at the soldier's hand that encircled my arm. It was big and red and beefy. And without a second thought, I bit down on it.

With a yelp of pain, the soldier pulled his hand away. As I sprang to freedom, the soldier yelled at me, "You little brat!"

The other soldier grabbed at me. But I slid around him and took hold of Leah's hand, pulling her behind me.

I was the fastest runner in my class, and I turned on the speed. We ran down one block and then another. I could hear Leah panting. But we didn't dare slow down.

I sneaked a look over my shoulder. No one seemed to be chasing us. But we still had to be careful.

We dodged down one alley and then another. Then I stopped and peered around the corner of a building. The coast was clear.

"You heard what the soldier said," Leah gasped out. "We can't hang around together anymore—it's too dangerous for you!" She gave me a little shove. "You better go home!"

"The Germans don't scare me," I said with a bravery I didn't really feel.

"It's dangerous for me too!" Leah said. She leaned back against the building, trying to catch her breath.

She was too thin. And her eyes were too large in her hollowed-out face. "If the Nazis catch a Jew disobeying them, they do all kinds of terrible things!" Leah said.

"It's so hard at home," she said. "Jews are no longer allowed to work, so we have no money. And even if we did, no one is allowed to sell us anything. We can't even buy any food! Once a week Papa walks out to the countryside to beg something from the farmers. Sometimes Mama goes too, and tries to trade her jewelry for food."

She paused and drew a long, shuddering breath. "Every time they go, I'm so afraid. I'm afraid that they'll be picked up and taken away!" she said.

I frowned. "Taken away where?" I asked.

Leah took my arm, drawing me toward her. I could feel her trembling. "The Nazis are taking more Jews all the time—right off the streets, right out of our houses and synagogues! The Nazis say they're taking Jews to work camps. To make parts for airplanes and tanks. But we've heard rumors that the camps are horrible, horrible places! That people are beaten and starved—and worse!" she cried.

Her words sent chills up and down my spine.

"That's why some of my friends have gone into hiding," Leah continued.

"What do you mean?" I asked.

"I mean, they just disappear," Leah said. "Christians hide them on their farms or in their attics or cellars. Some families even have secret rooms in their houses where they're hiding Jews. It's the only chance we have not to be sent to the camps."

"Will you go into hiding, Leah?" I asked.

She shrugged. "My parents said it would be too hard for our whole family to hide since my sister's still a baby," Leah said. "But they said that maybe I could go on my own. There's a family in the country that has a hiding place just big enough for one person."

She shook her head and said, "But I don't know, Annie. I don't know if I could do it. Hide all by myself—maybe for years—in a stranger's home."

"If it's your only chance, Leah, then you have to take it!" I urged.

"Maybe—I don't know," Leah said. She looked down. "Anyway, this will be the last time we see each other, Annie. Mrs. Van Kooten told us today that Jewish children are no longer allowed to go to public school. From now on we have to go to a Jewish school."

"I can come to your house," I said quickly, "or you can come to mine—" I stopped.

Of course we couldn't do that. We couldn't even be seen together anymore.

I squeezed Leah's hand and said, "It's only good-bye until the end of the war, Leah. Then we'll see each other again. And maybe by then we'll be old enough to go all those places we've talked about! Egypt and Africa!"

Leah's thin face lit up. "And Tasmania!" Her hand clutched at mine so tightly, I could feel her nails digging into my palms. "We'll go everywhere, Annie. Just like we said we would!"

"You're the smartest girl in our class, Leah." I spoke with all the firmness I could summon up. "If you have to go into hiding by yourself, you can do it!"

I threw my arms around Leah. "Promise me you'll do everything you can so you won't have to go to one of those camps. So that after the war, we can find each other again," I whispered.

"I promise, Annie," Leah said in a quiet voice. She unfastened the small, golden Star of David she wore on a chain around her neck. She held it out to me. "I want you to have this. So you'll always remember me," she said.

I quickly took off my tiny silver cross. I gave it to her. "And you take this," I said. "It will remind you that we're still best friends! No matter what!"

"No matter what," Leah echoed.

We were both silent a moment. Neither one of us was sure how to say good-bye. Then suddenly, Leah said, "We'll count to five, and then we'll say good-bye together, okay?"

I nodded. It was a good plan. It would make the last moment easier.

"Let's start," Leah said.

One. I thought of how long we'd known each other—since kindergarten.

Two. I thought of how we rode our bikes together. And went ice skating and roller skating. How we did everything together.

Three. I thought of how we told each other everything. All our secrets and all our hopes and dreams for the future.

Four. I thought of how much I was going miss her. And how I would never, ever have another friend like her.

Five. We said it together. Just like we'd planned. "Good-bye!"

I bit my lip to stop it from trembling. "See you after the war, Leah!" I said.

"After the war, Annie!" she returned.

We split apart and started running. I went one way, and Leah went another. Just like the Nazis wanted.

But as I ran, I remembered what Leah had said that day in the country. When I'd told her I wanted to keep the moment forever.

"You can," she'd said. "Your memories are always with you."

I stood in front of the bedroom door. It sounded like someone was crying. But it couldn't possibly be Siri!

For once I didn't go barging into the room my sister and I now shared. Instead, I knocked gently. "Siri?" I called.

"You can come in, Annie," Siri answered. She sounded as if she were far away.

She was curled up on the bed, knees drawn up to her chest. Her beautiful hair was spread around her like a silken shawl.

I'd never seen Siri like this before. What could possibly have gone wrong in her perfect life?

Slowly, Siri pushed up to a sitting position. When I cry, my face gets all red and splotchy. But Siri's skin was only softly flushed. Her eyes weren't puffy like mine would have been. They only gleamed more brightly. Yet in those crystal-blue eyes was a look I'd never seen before.

"What's wrong, Siri?" I asked softly.

She stood and walked to the window. "For the past year, Annie, I—I've been meeting a boy in secret. His name is Aaron," she said.

I couldn't even speak, I was so surprised! We both knew our mother's rules on going out with boys—it was strictly forbidden.

Oh, boys were allowed to walk Siri to and from church or choir practice. And once in a while they'd even been invited to the house for dinner. But to meet one alone—never! We had a reputation to maintain, Mama always said, as a minister's daughters.

"I met him over a year ago in the little warming house by the pond. I was skating, and so was he. We started talking and laughing," Siri said.

She turned to me. Her feelings for this Aaron lit her face like a candle. "He's so nice and funny and smart." She blushed. "And handsome!"

"Why didn't you ask him home to meet Papa and Mama?" I asked.

She lowered her head. "I know I should have. But . . . he's Jewish, Annie!" Siri said. "I was afraid that Mama might not approve. That she wouldn't think it was right for a minister's daughter to be seeing a Jewish boy. I wouldn't let him tell his parents about me either."

Siri continued, "And now Aaron's been rounded up and taken to a work camp! I was supposed to meet him this afternoon. At the same little warming house where we always went. But his sister came instead. Aaron asked her to tell me what had happened."

I remembered Leah's words about the camps. I couldn't tell Siri. Not now.

Still looking out the window, Siri said, "I know you think I'm all prim and proper—and perfect. That's what everyone thinks! But the truth is—" She turned to face me. "I'm just afraid to say what I really think or feel. Or do what I really want to. Afraid that I'll make someone mad at me. I wish I were brave like you, Annie! But I'm not."

I stared at Siri. At my slender, graceful, beautiful sister. She thought I was brave! She thought silly, messy, loud Annie was brave!

"If I'd been braver, maybe Aaron and I could have had a life together. No matter what anyone said," Siri continued. "And now . . . now it's too late."

Siri started crying again. I went to her. And as I had done when I was small, I began stroking her long hair. I didn't know what else to do. And I couldn't think of anything to say. I just wanted her to know that I was there for her.

And as we stood there, I tried to get over my surprise that Siri thought she should be something different than what she was. Just like I did. All at once I felt closer to my sister than ever before.

Rain started to splatter the windowpane. The kind of heavy rain that turned the whole world gray.

I could feel the rain inside me. Just as I'd felt the sunshine that day in the country. And it was like heavy sadness, pressing down on me from all sides. It seemed as if the whole world was weeping.

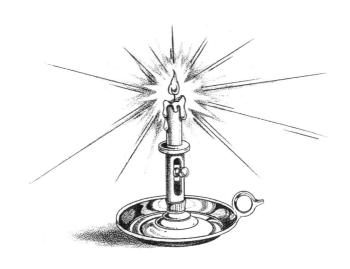

5

THE SECRET DOOR

"Papa!" My voice echoed eerily in the empty church. "Papa!"

It was way past the time my father had said he'd be home. Mama had sent me to the church to find him.

I knew the church as well as I knew our own house. But at night, lit only by my small candle, it looked like a completely different place.

Strange shadows leaped against the walls. And every little creak of the old, wooden beams made me jump. Doorways were black, yawning caves. And the furniture had become crouching animals, ready to spring out at me.

I held my candle high and peered down the rows of pews. I could smell candle wax and the beeswax that was used to polish the wood.

My father was definitely not here. Could he be in his office? Was he working so hard on his sermon that he didn't hear my calls? I turned and started for the stairs. I felt my way with one hand.

It was June 1942, and the Nazis had been in Holland for two years. Every day life grew harsher. We could only use electricity a few hours each day now. That's why I carried a candle. The Nazis took most of what our farmers produced to ship off to their troops. So everyone was low on food.

We were forbidden to sing our own national anthem. Even to hum it under our breath meant we could be dragged off to jail! The tires on my bicycle had worn down to nothing. But we couldn't replace them because the Nazis took everything our factories made. So like everyone else in Holland, I rode around on metal rims, clattering and bumping over our brick streets.

On the second floor, I called out again. "Papa!" No answer.

I opened the door to his office and looked around. His big chair was pushed back from a desk that was covered with papers and books. But the room was empty.

The Nazis had ordered an 8 p.m. curfew. To be out on the streets after that meant you could be picked up and taken to jail. It was well past 8:00 now. So surely

Papa hadn't gone anywhere else. But if he was still in the church, then where was he? It was all very strange.

That was when I heard it. A soft but steady noise was coming from behind the bookcase that stood against the back wall. Could it be mice?

I didn't run or scream at the thought of a mouse. Not like women did in the movies or stories. In fact, I thought I'd like to catch this noisy mouse and bring him home as a pet!

The noise grew louder. It began sounding almost like footsteps. It would have to be an enormous mouse to make that kind of sound! But if it wasn't a mouse . . . then what was it? Or who was it?

My heart started to pound.

Maybe there was a real mystery here, just waiting for me to uncover it. Or maybe I should turn around. Maybe I should run down the stairs and keep on running until I was back home. That would definitely be the safer thing.

Annie Van Vries, I told myself sternly, all your life you've been waiting for an adventure. And now when you just might have one, are you really going to turn tail and run? No!

I set down my candle and leaned one shoulder against the bookcase. I was trying to shove it away from the wall. With much groaning and grunting, I moved it a few feet.

That's when I noticed that the bookcase was hinged to the wall on the right side. But I could only see the hinges after moving the bookcase away from the wall. How strange!

Using the hinges, I swung the bookcase open to reveal a door. A secret door! In all the years Papa had been pastor at this church, I had never known this door was here. What could be behind it?

How I wished Leah were here. It would be more fun and exciting to have her with me. And less frightening. Together, we would open the door and go exploring!

But I was alone. And that's how I was going to have to solve this mystery. On my own.

I opened the door. On the other side was a steep, winding staircase. I went back into the office for my candle and then started up the stairway.

The noise had stopped. But I could feel that whatever or whoever had made the noise was still there—somewhere. Waiting.

I climbed the stairs. And the musty, unaired smell of a place that has been closed up for a long time was all around me. But oddly enough, I could also smell fresh paint.

The stairway ended in front of another door. Should I open it?

I turned the knob, but the door was locked. I knocked softly. No answer. I knocked more firmly.

Again, nothing. I started pounding. It probably wasn't a very wise thing to do, I thought. But it might get results.

As I pounded, I deepened my voice. I called out loudly and tried to sound official. "Open up!" I yelled. "I know you're in there!"

Maybe no one was in there. Or maybe someone was in there and my plan would backfire. Maybe the door would suddenly swing open and a hand would reach out and grab me! Maybe—

Very slowly, the door opened. Standing before me was Papa. And behind him stood a man, a woman, and a child. All three of them clung closely together, frozen in fear.

At the sight of me, Papa's eyes popped. "Annie!" he breathed. "It's all right, everyone," he called over his shoulder. "This is my younger daughter, Annie!"

The three people let out their breath in one big sigh of relief.

Quickly, Papa pulled me into the room. He shut the door behind him. I saw a kitchen table covered with a red tablecloth, a rocking chair, a small sink, and a gas stove.

"What are you doing here?" Papa asked.

"Mama sent me to find you," I stammered. "You weren't downstairs, so I came up here. I heard sounds from behind the bookcase. When I moved it, I saw the door—"

"And you just couldn't resist investigating," Papa finished. He shook his head. As he usually did when faced with one of my misadventures. "I should be angry. But I'm so glad it's you, I can't be anything but thankful!"

He gestured to the three people who stood silently watching. "These are the Sterns. Mr. and Mrs. Stern and their daughter, Ruth."

Suddenly, it all became clear. The Sterns were Jewish. And they were hiding behind the secret door, in this secret room, from the Nazis! It was just like Leah had explained.

I smiled at the little girl. "I thought maybe it was a family of giant mice behind the bookcase," I said. The girl giggled, and Mr. Stern smiled.

"Sorry to disappoint you," Mr. Stern said. His brown eyes lit up with laughter. "A family of larger-than-life mice would have been much more interesting!"

I like him, I thought. How brave he is! To be able to find humor in a place and at a time like this.

Mrs. Stern took my hand between both of hers in a warm clasp. "It's so nice to know you, Annie," she said. "It's an honor to meet anyone in Pastor Van Vries' family! He's a very special man."

"Yes," I agreed, "he is."

But Papa just made a motion with one hand as if to wave away the compliment. "I'm just doing what hundreds of Dutch people are doing," he said.

Then Papa looked at me. "Did you put the bookcase back, Annie?" he asked.

"No," I said, suddenly afraid. "I'm sorry—"

"It's all right. You couldn't know," Papa said. "But we'd better get it in place. Just in case anyone else comes wandering in." He took my arm and guided me out the door.

"I'll see you tomorrow," he called softly to the Sterns.

"Good-bye," I said over my shoulder. And then the door swung shut.

Back in his office, Papa sat down behind his desk. He motioned me into the smaller chair across from him. I knew this was how he sat when he helped people over the rough bumps in their lives.

The flickering light of the candle revealed how tired Papa looked. But his eyes, as always, were calm and warm.

"How long has the secret room been there, Papa?" I asked.

"Since the church was built," he answered. "There are three rooms, really. And they were meant to serve as a home for the pastor and his family. But the rooms are so tiny that it wasn't very practical."

Papa continued. "There's the kitchen, which you saw. The Sterns use it for a living room too. There's a foldaway bed in there that Mr. Stern sleeps on. Then there's a bedroom that Ruth and Mrs. Stern share. And there's a little water closet.

51

"After our home was built, the church just closed up the rooms," Papa went on. "People forgot about them. But when the Resistance asked me if I had room enough to hide a whole family, I suddenly remembered. I cleaned out the cobwebs and dust. And I even put on a fresh coat of paint."

"That's why you've been gone so much," I said quickly. "And you have all those meetings behind closed doors, when you all speak in a whisper!"

I knew I'd just given away my snooping. But I didn't care. I was too busy fitting the pieces of this puzzle together. "You're in the Resistance!" I said.

I should have figured it out before, I thought. Of course, Papa would have joined the band of people who worked secretly against the Nazis.

I leaned forward eagerly. "Tell me all about it!" I begged.

Papa took his pipe from his pocket. He couldn't get tobacco anymore. But he still liked to have his pipe close by. I knew when he was worrying or thinking over a problem because he'd hold the pipe to his mouth and chew on the stem. Now he leaned back in his chair and began turning the pipe over in his hands.

"I can't tell you everything, Annie. If you're ever taken in for questioning, it's best that you not know too much," Papa said. "But I can tell you some things. My Resistance unit meets every day at the same time. We always meet at the same place, a shop owned by one of our members. That way, if one of us doesn't show up, the rest of us know that something's happened. We know not to do anything for a few days. But no matter what, we always start up again!"

"What sorts of things do you do?" I asked.

"Some people in the Resistance disable the Nazis' cars and trucks. Or steal their guns. Or even blow up their tanks!" Papa explained. "But the group I'm with finds hiding places for Jewish people. We even have our own printing press hidden in a cellar. We print up ration cards that we give to Christians hiding Jews. We have Jews hidden everywhere. In nursing homes and hospitals, and offices and attics."

Papa made a clenched fist out of one hand. "It's not just Jews who have to go into hiding. It's anybody the Nazis consider an enemy!" He began to pound his fist on the desk. "If you love Holland or think people have a right to be free, the Nazis will come after you!"

Papa paused. But his fist remained clenched. And on his face was written how much he hated the Nazis and what they stood for. And what they had done to his country.

"How long have the Sterns been hiding here?" I asked.

"Only a few days," Papa answered. "The Resistance just got word that the Nazis are planning to round up every Jewish man, woman, and child and send them to work camps. We've had to move very quickly to get as many as we could into hiding."

"Papa," I said slowly, "what happens if the Nazis find out you're in the Resistance?"

"They'll arrest me," Papa said. He was very matter-of-fact. "And then I'll be sent to a work camp too."

I shivered at the very thought of Papa being taken away. I couldn't bear to think of him being mistreated. And how would I ever make it through the war without him?

"I want to help the Sterns too," I said.

Papa opened his mouth to protest. But I went quickly on. "I love Holland too. And freedom! I want to feel like I'm fighting back—at least a little!" I said.

The image of Leah's frightened face came into my mind. "If I could help the Sterns, it would be like doing something for Leah," I said quietly.

Papa stared at me. It seemed as if his eyes were going deep down into my soul. Right to the very core of who I was.

"You're right, Annie," Papa said finally. "You should help. I have to remember that you're not a little girl anymore. You've had to grow up very quickly in these past few years. But you have to understand. You must never, never tell anyone about the Sterns and the secret room."

"I understand, Papa. I can keep a secret!" I promised.

"You can certainly find out secrets!" Papa said.

We both smiled at his words.

"You mustn't even tell your mother," Papa said. He frowned and went on slowly. It was as if he was searching for just the right way to say what he had to.

"Your mother is a person who needs order in her life," he explained. "It scares her when things don't go just as she thinks they should. That's why she gets so upset when you—or I—break the rules. Especially the ones the Nazis have set down. If she found out about the Sterns . . . well, it would be more than she could bear."

"Can I tell Siri?" I asked.

"The fewer people that know, the safer it will be. So for the time being, let's not say anything to her either," Papa said.

Papa stood. Taking my hand, he pulled me to my feet. Then again he looked deep into my eyes. It was as if he were trying to imprint his words on my mind. "Never forget this, Annie. From now on, the lives of those three people depend on us!"

6

TRUE FREEDOM

"Say it all over again, Annie," Ruth commanded me. She was sitting with her eyes shut.

Once again I began to describe how it looked outside. I told her how blue the sky was. That the clouds looked as soft and fluffy as ice cream. And that the wind carried the smell of flowers and the scent of the sea.

She sighed with pleasure. Then she opened her eyes and picked up one of the crayons. She bent her head over the paper. And she began to draw what I had just described.

Ruth so longed to go outside. She wasn't able to run and play. Or feel the wind on her back and the sun on her face. So instead, we'd made up this game.

Every day when I came to visit, I would tell her what it was like outside. Then she would draw it.

Ruth was a wonderful artist! She drew pictures of everything and everyone. Flowers, the canal, funny pictures of her father and mother, Papa, and me.

Ruth loved to tell me about the apartment they'd had in Amsterdam. She talked about her old school. I heard about her grandmother with the warm laugh and comfy lap. The Sterns had moved to Holland from Germany when things started getting bad there for the Jews. Ruth said they'd begged her grandmother to come to Holland with them. But she'd said she was too old for so much change. Every day, Ruth said, the Sterns prayed that her grandmother was safe.

I learned that Ruth loved to play the piano. And that she'd had a kitten named Daisy. But she had to leave her behind when they went into hiding. She still cried sometimes when she talked about Daisy. And she drew lots of pictures of her.

I discovered that Mrs. Stern was a very good cook. I also discovered that if she really liked you—and she really liked me—she'd pinch your cheek and give you a hug every time she saw you!

Mrs. Stern was as round as a dumpling and soft as a feather pillow. Or at least, she had been. Like everyone else in Holland, she was getting thinner and thinner.

Every day there were longer and longer lines in front of the butcher's shop. And at the vegetable and fruit stands. Food was getting much harder to find. We only had one forged ration card to feed all three Sterns.

Papa never let me buy the food for the Sterns. He said there was always the chance that the Nazis would discover it was a false card. And he didn't want me in that kind of danger. But he did let me walk out to the country with him to try to find food.

The farmers were always generous. But sometimes they had very little to share. Once in a while Papa and I would come back with some eggs or—miracle of miracles—a scrawny chicken! But usually it was onions, beets, and carrots. And, if we were lucky, a few potatoes.

Whatever we found, we divided equally between our family and the Sterns. Mrs. Stern could make the most wonderful stews and soups out of almost nothing.

Mr. Stern always seemed to be laughing at something. His kind eyes crinkled at the corners when he smiled. And he was really smart.

Papa was always bringing him books to read. And Mr. Stern liked to help me with my math and science. I liked it too! For the first time since Leah had left, my grades in those subjects started to improve.

I told Ruth all about Leah. Ruth drew Leah's picture too. And she told me about her own friends.

As Ruth talked, she drew. And as she drew, I thought what a pretty little girl she was. With her big dark eyes and her black hair tumbling around her shoulders. She'll be beautiful, I thought, when she grows up. If the Nazis let her grow up . . .

The Sterns had to stay completely quiet all day

long. If they wanted to walk from room to room, they had to do so in stocking feet. They couldn't flush the toilet or run water if there was anyone in the church besides Papa and me.

Papa and I could never go up to see them if there was anyone else in the building. And the Sterns could never take the chance and come down the stairs—ever. We all knew that we couldn't slip up. Not even once. Because if we did, it might mean the Nazis would discover the hiding place.

I wondered how the Sterns managed to live with all that fear. And I felt that one of my duties was to keep their spirits up. Whenever I entered their little home, I put a smile on my face and pretended that all was well.

They had enough to worry about. I couldn't let on just how badly things were going for the Jews in the outside world. Or how poor and hungry the Dutch people were becoming.

I went to see the Sterns every day. I'd make sure the church was empty and the curtains on the office window were drawn. Then I'd swing open the bookcase, open the secret door, and climb the steep, winding stairs.

If Mama ever asked where I was, I'd just say I was at the church. I'd tell her I was getting extra help on my homework. And I was. Only not from Papa.

It was funny. I actually enjoyed my quiet times with Ruth. She couldn't replace Leah, of course. No one could. But in gentle, thoughtful Ruth, I found someone to talk with. And to share my plans for the future with.

I brought over Papa's maps. And Ruth and I found all the places I wanted to go after the war—and some new ones too!

Mr. Stern had planned a course of study for Ruth so she wouldn't get too behind in her schoolwork. And together, we did our homework.

We worked puzzles together too, and read to each other. Ruth even taught me to draw. Me—Annie Van Vries with her clumsy fingers!

Sometimes while Ruth drew, I would write down all the things I'd seen that day. All the things that had happened and my feelings about them. I even wrote poems! Funny poems about the trouble I got into. And longer poems about the sea.

I learned a lot during my visits to the Sterns'. I learned that I didn't always have to rush around to have fun. I discovered that inside my head was a whole world just waiting to be explored! A world of exciting thoughts and fascinating new ideas.

The new things I was learning and finding out about myself carried over to school too. Mrs. Van Kooten told me that I was starting to soak up facts and figures like a sponge!

Papa visited the Sterns once a day as well. He brought them food and news about the outside world that wouldn't upset them. He was gone from home more and more all the time.

I knew he was busy with the Resistance. On the surface, Papa was a Dutch Reformed pastor in a small village. He was just a man who visited the sick, gave sermons, and helped people with their problems. But underneath, he was part of a web of secret fighters that stretched all over Holland.

The more Papa was gone, the more Mama worried. And the more she worried, the more she yelled.

When she shouted at me that my bed was unmade or my socks needed pulling up, I tried to remember what Papa had said. That Mama was a woman who needed order in her life to be happy. And now all order and peace were gone. I tried to remember, too, that she wasn't really angry when she shouted at me. She was just afraid.

It was then that I tried to use what I had learned at the Sterns'. I would go up to my bedroom and let a book carry me to faraway places. Or I would write a poem about what I was feeling. Or draw a picture. And then the next day I would show Ruth my work.

Mama started to notice this new side of noisy Annie. "I have two well-mannered daughters now," Mama said to me one day, looking up from her mending.

She patted the sofa beside her. And I sat down and snuggled up to her like when I was small. She put down her needle and thread to take my chin in her hands. "You're turning into a pretty girl, Annie," she said. "Of course, you don't look like Siri."

My heart sank. No matter what, Mama still wanted me to be like my sister.

But then Mama went on. "You look like yourself. And that's a very good thing to be!"

I couldn't believe my ears! Mama liked me—loved me—for who I was.

Part of me would always love running and jumping. And making noise and giving people fits. But now I knew I had another side as well.

And for my discovery of that new part of me, I had three people hiding behind a secret door to thank. Every time I went into their little home, the Sterns always thanked me for my help. But I knew I was receiving much more than I was giving.

The only window in the Sterns' small apartment was in the bedroom. It was set high up in the wall. And Ruth and I liked to lie back on the floor and peer up through the window at the sky. Sometimes we would open the window and let the fresh air wash over us as we watched the clouds.

Ruth especially loved watching the seagulls. "Look how they dip and soar, Annie," she said one day. "I wonder what it would feel like to fly!"

"I used to think about that," I said. "How wonderful it would be to go wherever you wanted!"

I paused, watching the gulls in flight. "They look like white lights, don't they?" I said. "They fly by your window like flashes of freedom."

Suddenly Ruth sat up, wrapping her thin arms around her drawn-up knees. Her voice was thick with fear and loneliness. "If I were a seagull, I could fly out of Holland. Over the ocean—to America. Then I'd be free too!"

I sat up and put one arm around Ruth's shoulders. "I've learned so many things from coming to visit you," I said. "From watching and listening to you and your family, I've learned you can create a whole world in your mind. I've learned that you can imagine yourself anywhere you want to be. And that if you go deep inside to your own thoughts, no one can get you there. Not the Nazis. Not anyone!"

I smiled at Ruth, and she leaned her head on my shoulder. Together, we watched the seagulls for a few minutes.

Then reaching right into my heart for the words, I went on. I felt very wise and grown-up at that moment.

I said to Ruth, "Deep inside, in your own spirit—that's where you'll find true freedom!"

7

THE KNOCK ON THE DOOR

I jumped out of bed and looked out the window. The sky was the kind of clear blue that only comes in October. Cloudless and shining. No rain—and no school!

It was Saturday. And after I did my morning chores, I could spend the rest of the day just as I pleased.

The Nazis took all our coal to ship back to Germany. So in our village, like in the rest of Holland, we'd had to chop down most of our beautiful trees for firewood.

But there were still a few left. And on those, the leaves were turning wonderful shades of red and gold. I couldn't wait to tell Ruth all about it!

I got dressed as quickly and quietly as I could. I was trying not to disturb Siri. I ran down the stairs and headed for the kitchen and breakfast.

"Good morning, Mama, Papa!" I said. I slid out my chair and was just about to sit down when we heard the knock on the door.

"Who could be coming to see you so early?" Mama asked as she stood working at the stove.

Papa shook his head. "I don't have an appointment with anyone," he answered.

The knock came again. But as Papa stood up, it turned into angry pounding.

"Open up!" The words came out in an impatient rush of German-accented Dutch. "Open this door immediately!"

I saw Papa stagger. He grabbed a chair to steady himself. His eyes met mine. Had the Nazis found out about the secret room? Was that why they were here?

"Germans," Mama whispered. She collapsed into a chair as if her legs would no longer support her. "What will we do?" she muttered, sounding like a child again. Just as she had on the night of the bombing. "What will we do?"

Papa pulled himself up straight. Very calmly, he walked to the door. "We will let them in, of course," he said in a voice that only shook a little bit. "What else can we do?"

Papa threw open the door. A Nazi soldier burst in. And on the stoop behind him, I could see two more soldiers.

Tears of fright gathered at the back of my throat. It felt like there was a cold, clenched fist in the pit of my stomach.

"Are you Pastor Peter Van Vries?" the soldier asked in a harsh voice.

"I am," Papa answered steadily.

The soldier barked out orders. "Then you have ten minutes to pack a bag and come with us!"

"No!" Mama wailed. She jumped up and ran to the soldier. "My husband has done nothing wrong! Oh, there was that day when he wore the yellow flower. But that's all! He's a good man—ask anyone!"

Mama grabbed the soldier by both arms. "You can't take him—you can't! What will I do? What will our daughters do? What will the church do?" she cried.

The soldier shoved Mama away roughly. He yelled at her, "Shut up!"

Mama stumbled and fell to her knees. Quickly, Papa tried to go to her. But the soldier barred the way with his rifle butt.

I ran to Mama and put my arms around her. "It's all right," I said, not knowing where my voice came from. I helped Mama to her feet.

"But why?" Mama sobbed. "Why are you taking my husband?"

"We've had our eye on Pastor Van Vries since the day he tore the sign down in the square," the soldier snapped. "And we've discovered that he's not quite the man he pretends to be. He's a member of the Resistance!"

Mama went pale. I could feel her shaking in my arms. "No," she whispered.

The soldier prodded Papa in the stomach with his rifle. "I gave you an order—get going! You have ten minutes!"

Slowly, as if gathering his strength, Papa turned and started up the stairs.

"We have to help Papa now," I said to my mother. I made my words firm and clear, as if speaking to a child.

"Help Papa," Mama repeated, and I nodded. I took her arm. And together, we followed Papa upstairs.

Siri was standing at the bedroom door. She was dressed, hairbrush in hand. And the look in her eyes was like that of a frightened animal.

Papa took a small suitcase out of his closet. "I'm all ready," he said, smiling sadly. "I knew the Nazis would be coming for me sooner or later. And I didn't want to waste any time packing."

He pulled Mama from me and held her close. "I promise you, Valerie, I will come home again. I'm strong. I can take whatever they do to me!"

Papa held Mama out at arms' length. "Your job when I'm gone will be the same as always. To take care of the girls and keep the house up. Do you understand?" Papa asked.

Mama nodded.

Papa continued, "Will you promise me you'll do those things so I won't worry?"

"I promise, Peter," Mama said in a voice as small as a child's.

"Good," Papa said. He motioned to my sister to come and take Mama.

"Your job, Siri, will be to take care of your mother. Will you do that for me?" Papa asked.

"Of course I will," Siri answered.

How wise Papa is, I thought. Giving Mama a sense of order. And giving them both things to do when he was gone. Things to hang on to.

"You can start now," Papa said to Siri. "I think we have just enough coffee left for one strong cup! Take Mama downstairs now and make her some coffee, all right?"

Siri put her slender, graceful arms around Mama and led her to the door. But then she stopped and looked back at Papa. "I love you," Siri said in her soft, gentle voice.

Papa lifted one hand in farewell. "And I love you, Siri."

As soon as Siri and Mama had gone, Papa turned to me. He was serious. But he didn't seem afraid or rushed. Even now, Papa was still the calm center in the eye of the storm.

"The Nazis didn't mention the Sterns, so I don't think they've found out," he said. He put his hands on my shoulders. And I could almost feel his strength flowing into me. "I always said you were meant for some special purpose, and this is it! You must take care of the Sterns! Your Mama could never do it. Nor Siri either. It is you I'm counting on!"

"Remember that day in the square?" I asked Papa. My words were coming out all topsy-turvy and full of feeling. "When you said these are the kinds of times that make people wonder what they're made of? Well, now I know I'm made of the same stuff you are— good, strong Dutch stubbornness. You can count on me, Papa!"

Papa smiled, and I saw tears sparkling in his eyes. He drew me into a hug so fierce it took my breath away.

For just a moment I clung to him. Then he let me go. He picked up his bag and went to the door. When I started to follow, he held out a hand to stop me.

"No, I want you to stay here," Papa said. "I want to remember you just as you are now." His lips trembled, but he didn't break. And neither would I. "Good-bye, Annie," Papa said. And then he was gone.

I stood stock-still in the center of the bedroom. I was waiting for the sound of the front door closing to tell me Papa was gone. I felt the slam like a shudder in my own body.

I ran to the window and watched. One of the soldiers shoved Papa onto a truck where several other men sat hunched over. They must be in Papa's Resistance unit, I thought.

When I heard the truck start up, I shut my eyes. Papa was gone. I wouldn't be able to make it without him. I grabbed tightly onto the window ledge.

No, I told myself, gritting my teeth. No! I *am* strong enough. I have to be!

That night I brought Siri to the secret rooms. She stared at the family and their rooms as if she couldn't believe what she was seeing. The Sterns stared shyly at her too. As if they couldn't believe her beauty.

"She looks like a fairy princess," Ruth whispered.

"I think so too," I answered. And I suddenly realized I wasn't jealous. My sister had her good points. But now I knew that I did too!

Siri and I were different. Everyone in the world was different! And that was all right. It was better than all right; it was good. Better than good! It was just as it should be. Because we each had our own strengths. Our own specialness.

Siri wouldn't be visiting the Sterns every day. That

would make Mama too suspicious. But she would be able to help me find food and the other things the family needed. She would be someone to lean on.

"I'll do the best I can, Annie," she'd said seriously when I told her about the secret door and the family in hiding. "I'm trying to learn how to be brave from you."

Imagine that, I thought. Siri is learning something from me! As I had learned something from the Sterns.

"I want to help the Sterns," Siri finished. "It will be a little like doing something for Aaron."

And Leah, I thought. . . .

Before I left the secret rooms that night, I took something from my pocket. It was the little white flower Papa had given me the day the Nazis marched into our village. I had carefully pressed it in a book.

Now I opened Ruth's hand and put the flower in her palm. I closed her fingers over it as Papa had done with me.

"My father gave me this flower," I said. "And now I give it to you. It's a flower of hope!"

Our house seemed empty and echoing that first night without Papa. Siri and I could hear Mama crying in her bedroom. And Siri went to comfort her. It would be hard for the three of us. And for the Sterns too.

They had depended on Papa. They'd had confidence in him. Now their lives depended on a 15-year-old girl.

But I wouldn't let them down! After all, wasn't I slippery as an eel and twice as clever—the best spy in Holland?! I would keep them safe—and Mama and Siri too—until the war was over!

I opened the top drawer in the dresser Siri and I shared. And I took out the necklace Leah had given me.

I missed her so much. Just like I would miss Papa. But they weren't really gone from me, I told myself. No more than I was gone from them.

I walked to the window. Wherever they were right now, I knew that they could hear me. Not with their ears, but with their hearts. Which is the best and truest way to hear anyone.

And so I put my face against the windowpane, whispering into the dark of the night. Whispering to Papa and Leah, and to myself. "Our memories are always with us."